John Townsend Trowbridge

The Lost Earl

with other poems and tales in verse

John Townsend Trowbridge

The Lost Earl
with other poems and tales in verse

ISBN/EAN: 9783337089528

Printed in Europe, USA, Canada, Australia, Japan

Cover: Foto ©Andreas Hilbeck / pixelio.de

More available books at **www.hansebooks.com**

THE LOST EARL

WITH OTHER POEMS AND

TALES IN VERSE

BY

JOHN TOWNSEND TROWBRIDGE

ILLUSTRATED

BOSTON
D LOTHROP COMPANY
FRANKLIN AND HAWLEY STREETS

CONTENTS.

APOLOGY   11

THE LOST EARL   13

HOW THE KING LOST HIS CROWN.   19

MY CAREER   22

CAPTAIN SEABORN   ,   29

SENATOR GRANDILOW .   41

"WHEN WE CAME HOME FROM THE WAR"   45

THE KANSAS FARMER .   48

A MOTHER'S TRAGEDY   53

AFTER THE SALE .   63

THREE WORLDS   75

THE SEEKING .   84

HYMN OF THE AIR   88

THE POET .   94

AT MOUNT DESERT   103

CONTENTS.

THE BELL-BUOY AT MOUNT DESERT   .   111

THE CABIN   119

ODE   122

AFTER THE CONCERT .   125

QUATRAINS AND EPIGRAMS   128

WIDOW BROWN'S CHRISTMAS .   134

ILLUSTRATIONS.

1. "Could we think with his thoughts as he rides in the shadow
   That falls from the foothills — " . . . . *Frontis.*

2. " 'Taboo! taboo!' Too late the call:
   The clumsy idol fell at once
   Against the mummies on the wall," etc. . . . . Page 39

3.   — "All
   Swept out by the sheriff's sale."   Page 64

4. " She entered, a young man's happy bride,
   She crowned his home with hope and pride,
   And now goes forth by an old man's side,
           A weary wanderer." . . . . Page 73

5. " A dismal, dolorous sound,
     You would say, heard anywhere,
     Be the weather foul or fair." . . . . Page 116

6. " Setting forth, in column and row,
   Whatever a penny of gain can show." . . . . . . Page 134

7. " 'Ho! ho! wa'al, wa'al! that's a queer idee!
   That's a curi's ca'calation!' " . . . . Page 148

NOTE.— For the illustrations which accompany "Widow Brown's Christmas" the publishers are indebted to the courtesy of Messrs. Harper & Brothers.

THE LOST EARL

WITH OTHER POEMS AND TALES IN VERSE

APOLOGY.

I ask my soul why, day and night,
I pore and ponder and indite.

Vainly, my life long, I have sought
To find some utterance for my thought,
By lip or pen, by word or token,
To speak what in me lies unspoken;
My tongue gives freely all the rest,
But locks the sweetest and the best.

I lived remote, I labored long,
In tale and rhyme, romance and song,
To sow that seed of heavenly wheat
That tortures me with inward heat.
I grasp, I reach to deeps internal,
I scatter forth the fiery kernel;
In vain projected, it returns,
And in my bosom beats and burns.

The uttered word falls cold and dead,
The living word is still unsaid.
And should it be my fate forever
To fail, in ceaseless fond endeavor,
To sow the soul's exhaustless seed,
And reach to deeps that still recede,
I still, by eldest law, must choose
The blissful thraldom of the Muse,
Bend all to her imperious will,
And still her last commands fulfill.

THE LOST EARL.

WITH his lariat coiled on the horn of his sad-
        dle,
    Face bearded and bronzed, in the broad-shadowed
        hat ;
High boot-tops, and fringed leather leggings astraddle
    His bronco's brown sides ; pistol-belt, and all that ;
His shout ringing out, a bluff, resonant basso,
    Above the herd's bellowing ; hand that can hurl
At a gallop the long-looped and wide-swinging
        lasso, —
    There rides — can you fancy ? — the son of an
        earl.

With the best and the worst a familiar companion ;
    Who often in winter, at twenty below,
While guarding his cattle within the deep cañon,
    Camps down in his blanket, rolled up on the snow ;
Bold rider and roper, to aid in a round-up,
    Head off a stampede, run the ringleaders down :
In him — does he pause to remember ? — are bound
        up
    The hopes of a race of old knightly renown.

The world's pampered minion, he yet, in requital
    Of all its proud favors, could fling them aside
As a swimmer his raiment, shed riches and title,
    And plunge into life, breast the turbulent tide!
Some caprice, you infer, or a sudden declension
    Of fortune, the cause?   Rather say, the revolt
Of a strong native soul against soulless convention,
    And privilege shared by the roué and dolt.

He chafed at the gilded constraints of his station,
    The bright ball-and-chain of the name that he bore ;
Grew sick of the smiles of discreet adulation,
    That worshiped, not worth, but the honors men wore.
With falsities stifled, with flatteries sated,
    He loathed, as some player, his wearisome part,
The homage of lips where he righteously hated,
    The rank that forbade him the choice of his heart.

(For that choice, it is told, fell to one far below him
    In station, who yet was so loyal and true
In the love which he won, she could love and forego him,
    And even his nobleness nobly outdo ;
Who scorned to climb up to a class that would scorn to
    Receive her its peer ; and refusing to dim
The coronet's brightness her brow was not born to,
    Lived maidenly faithful to love and to him.)

Was it then, in despair at the pitiful wrangle
  His preference raised, he resolved to be free,
To escape from his toils, break the tyrannous tangle
  Of custom and caste, of descent and degree?
In this lot which he chose, has he sometimes repented
  The impulse that urged him? In scenes such as
      these,
Hard lodgment, hard fare, has he never lamented
  The days of relinquished enjoyment and ease?

Was that impulse a fault? Would he speak, would
      he tell us
  His sober conclusion! For good or for ill,
There are tides of the spirit which sometimes impel us,
  Sub-currents, more potent than reason and will,
That out of our sordid conditions uplift us,
  And make our poor common humanity great.
We toy with the helm, but they draw us, they drift
      us.
  They shape the deep courses of life and of fate.

But then comes regret, when the ebb leaves us
      stranded
  In doubt and disaster: was such his reward?
How much we might gain would the fellow be candid,
  This volunteer ranchman who might be a lord!

Could we think with his thoughts as he rides in the
    shadow
That falls from the foothills when, suddenly chill,
Far over the mesas of lone Colorado
    The fast-creeping twilight spreads solemn and still.

From the rose-tinted, snow-covered peaks, the bright
    sources
    Of torrents and rivers, the glow pales away ;
Through cañons and gulches the wild watercourses
    Rush hurried and hoarse : just the time, you would
        say,
For our exile to fall into sombre reflection, —
    The scion of earls, from the uppermost branch
Of the civilized tree, in its cultured perfection,
    Set here in the desolate life of the ranch !

Amid wastes of gray sagebrush, of grama and bunch-
    grass ;
    The comrade of cowboys, with souls scarce above
The level of driven dumb creatures that munch grass ;
    Self-banished from paths of preferment and love,
An unreturned prodigal, mumbling his husk :
    At least so your sapient soul has divined,
As he gallops far off and forlorn through the dusk.
    But little men know of a man's hidden mind.

In his jacket he carries a thumbed pocket Homer,
  To con at odd spells as he watches his herd;
And at times, in his cottage, (but that's a misnomer;
  A hut with one room!) you may hear, on my word.
These cool summer twilights, (in moments not taken
  For washing his dishes or darning his socks,)
On strings deftly thrummed a strange music awaken,
  Mazurka of Chopin's, sonata of Bach's.

As over the wide-shouldered Rockies the gleam
  Of day yet illumines the vastness and distance
Of snow-hooded summits, so shines the still beam
  Of high thought, high resolve, on his lonely existence.
(And a maiden, they say, of her own sweet accord.
  Who to-night may be sailing the moonlighted sea.
To the ranchman brings what she denied to the lord.
  Idle rumor, no doubt.   But, however it be) —

Our knight of the lasso, long-lineaged Norman,
  Now guiding his herd to good pasture and drink,
Now buying and selling, stock-owner and foreman,
  Feels life fresh and strong; well content, as I think,
That the world of traditional leisure and sport
  Without him should amble its indolent round.
Though lost to his title, to kindred and court,
  Here first in rude labor his manhood is found.

His conclusion is this, or I sadly mistake it :
   " To each his own part ; rugged action for me !
Be men, and not masks ; fill your sphere or forsake it.
   Use power and wealth ; but 'tis time to be free
When the trappings of life prove a burden and fetter.
   The walls of my forefathers' castle are stanch,
But a cabin, with liberty, shelters me better.
   Be lord of your realm, be it earldom or ranch ! "

HOW THE KING LOST HIS CROWN.

THE King's men, when he had slain the boar,
  Strung him aloft on the fisher's oar,
And, two behind and two before,
In triumph bore him along the shore.
    "An oar!" says the King: "'tis a trifle! — why
    Did the fisher frown and the good wife sigh?"
    "A trifle, sire!" was the Fool's reply:
    "Then frown or laugh who will: for I,
    Who laugh at all and am only a clown,
        Will never more laugh at trifles!"

A runner next day leaped down the sand,
And launched a skiff from the fisher's strand;
For he cried, — "An army invades the land!
The passes are seized on either hand!
    And I must carry my message straight
    Across the lake to the castle gate!"
    The castle he neared, but the waves were great,
    The fanged rocks foamed like jaws of Fate;
    And lacking an oar the boat went down.
        The Furies laugh at trifles!
19

The swimmer against the waves began
To strive, as a valiant swimmer can.
" Methinks," said the Fool, " 'twere no bad plan
If succor were sent to the drowning man ! "
  To succor a perilled pawn instead,
  The monarch, moving his rook ahead, —
  Bowed over the chessmen, white and red, —
  Gave " Check ! " — then looked on the lake and
    said,
  " The boat is lost, the man will drown ! "
    O King ! beware of trifles !

To the lords and mirthful dames the bard
Was trolling his latest song ; the guard
Were casting dice in the castle yard ;
And the captains all were drinking hard.
  Then came the chief of the halberdiers,
  And told to the King's astounded ears :
  " An army on every side appears !
  An army with banners and bows and spears !
  They have gained the wall and surprised the
    town ! "
    Our fates are woven of trifles !

The red usurper reached the throne ;
The tidings over the realm were blown ;

And, flying to alien lands alone
With a trusty few, the King made moan.
    But long and loudly laughed the Clown:
    " We broke the oar and the boat went down,
    And so the messenger chanced to drown:
    The messenger lost, we lost the town;
    And the loss of the town has cost a crown;
        And all these things are trifles!"

MY CAREER.

MY mother, they said, was a soldier's child;
  My father played in the band.
She was pretty and gay, he was handsome and wild,
  And she gave him her foolish hand.
He owed so much that he couldn't pay,
He borrowed some more and they ran away;
But my poor mother, whom he outran,
Put up at an almshouse, where began
   (I think I never just knew the year)
     My career —
   My extraordinary career!

He ran so well she lost his track
  In the little delay I made;
He ran so far he never came back,
  And there, of course, we stayed;
And, while the decrepit old pauper wives
Tossed me about, she brightened the knives,
And set the table, and swept the floor,
And scrubbed as she never had scrubbed before;
   But still watched over, with many a tear,
     My career —
   The beginning of my career!

22

In lap, or cradle, or on all-fours,
    I thrived, and made my way,
And tumbled about the poor-house doors,
    Till a lady came, one day,
A wealthy widow, who begged for me.
"I want your beautiful boy," says she,
"To fill the place of the one I have lost.
I will love him and rear him, and spare no cost
    To form his mind, and give him, my dear,
        A career —
    Maybe a distinguished career!"

My mother took on at a terrible rate,
    And called it a sin and a shame;
She would keep her darling in spite of fate;
    But consented, all the same.
To the widow's she went, and left me there,
Then fled in despair, I never knew where,
A childless mother, to mourn and roam;
While I had luxury, friends, and a home,   .
    With everything that could aid and cheer
        My career —
    My fortunate career!

My friends were as kind as friends could be,
    And they gave me teachers and books;

But I never could see their use to me,
  With fine clothes and good looks,
Money to spend, and a fortune still
Awaiting me in the widow's will.
So, very possibly, I looked down
On the poor, industrious youths in town,
    And followed, as proud as a prince or peer,
      My career —
    Already a gay career!

I could drive and dress and dance and dine,
  With exquisite grace and dash;
My taste was fine in horses and wine,
  And I sported a sweet moustache.
The widow, no doubt, sometimes complained
Of the rather high tone which I maintained,
My talents wasted and youth misspent,
And wept at the way her money went;
    For, though it was pleasant, I own 'twas dear:
      My career
    Was a pretty high-toned career!

" I have lost a bet! I must pay this debt!"
  I coaxed; she couldn't refuse.
A genteel fellow sometimes will get
  Into scrapes, and where's the use

Of having a fussy old woman about,
Who can't, or won't help a fellow out ?
I rushed from her presence a hundred times,
And threatened to plunge into horrid crimes,
    To end as a robber or buccaneer
        My career —
    My desperate career !

It was long to wait for a grand estate,
    But I was in luck at last.
I was tall and straight, I was twenty-eight,
    And, though a trifle fast,
A party the girls were mad to catch !
Considered a most amazing match
By smiling mammas and bowing papas,
And a deucedly delicate thing it was,
    With sirens on every side, to steer
        My career —
    Safely my free career !

For why should I marry, and have the care
    Of children and a wife ?
'Twas burden enough, by George ! to bear
    My own light butterfly life —
A thing I never could understand !
With fashion and wealth, gay friends at hand,

No thought for another, there weighed on me
Sometimes such weariness and ennui
    As few would have fancied could come near
        My career —
    My enviable career!

Yet I should state that I chose a mate,
    For a very good cause, indeed.
It was rather late; I was forty-eight;
    My moustache had gone to seed;
And, worst of all, one day I found
My fortune was high and dry aground!
So I looked about, resolved to win
Some widow, as rich as my first had been,
    From the rubbish of beggarly debts to clear
        My career —
    My really superb career!

Too lucky by half, I may say it now,
    Was I when I went to woo.
I didn't get on so well, somehow,
    With Widow Number Two.
A woman of taste, she couldn't but be
In love with an elegant man like me;
But she was a shrew, and she soon took fright,
Drew her prim lips and her purse-strings tight,

And eyed with an eye quite too severe
        My career —
Jealous of my career!

She scrimped me up and she screwed me down,
        In a most ridiculous way.
For a man of renown, the beau of the town,
        'Twas extremely little pay.
There never was husband fond as I —
Particularly when she came to die;
But in her will she was cruel still,
And cut me off with a codicil —
        Pulled up, of a sudden, as will appear,
                My career —
        My fashionable career!

Of the schemes I tried when drifting about
        There's little enough to tell.
As a mixer of fancy drinks, no doubt,
        I might have succeeded well.
I had no other art or trade;
And the fine, rich friends I asked for aid
Grew cold, scarce deigning at times to use
A word of pity or poor excuse;
        But viewing with secret glee, I fear,
                My career —
        My steady down-hill career!

My buttoned coat had a hungry look ;
    I sponged from bar to bar ;
Whoever would trust or treat, I took
    A glass or a bad cigar.
Homeless, alone, I walked the street ;
The old faces now that I chanced to meet
Passed by, with a smile at my altered style,
My tight cravat, and my battered tile ;
    And jubilant youngsters turned to jeer
        My career —
    My often zigzag career !

No need to relate what buffets of fate
    I afterward underwent.
I am feeble of gait ; I am sixty-eight ;
    My back and my knees are bent.
To the passers-by I have held my hat ;
But, Heaven be thanked, there's an end of that.
To the poor-house I have come home, at last,
To the poor-house where my first years passed,
    Old and infirm, to finish here
        My career —
    My rather played-out career !

CAPTAIN SEABORN.

OUR ship went down, and not a boat
   Outrode the storm's intensity ;
But I alone was left afloat
   Upon the blue immensity :
My raft and I together lashed,
   The wild seas racing under us,
Till reefs uprose, and breakers dashed
   About us, blind and thunderous.

Still, like Mazeppa to his horse,
   I clung, while, half submerging me,
On foaming shoals with fearful force
   The winds and waves were urging me.
I swooned : I woke : my dim eyes glanced
   Upon a hideous rabblement
Of islanders that round me pranced
   With frantic yells and babblement.

Half-drowned they dragged me from the sea
   Up the white beach, and, seating me
Against a skull-encircled tree,
   Made ghastly signs of eating me.

29

The frizzled women crouched to look
  My body over curiously ;
The tattooed braves above me shook
  Their battle-axes furiously.

Forth from my sailor's pouch, to buy
  My life of those fell savages,
I drew such slight effects as I
  Had saved from the sea's ravages.
With thimble, coins, carved ivory ball,
  I flattered and invited them ;
A rusted jack-knife, most of all,
  Astonished and delighted them.

Then fruits they brought and mats they spread
  With singular celerity :
Not death I gained, but gifts instead,
  And cannibal prosperity.
I lived with them and learned their speech ;
  I curbed their fierce brutality,
And strove with simple truths to reach
  Their dim spirituality.

The arts of peace, the love of right,
  I tried to teach ; economy
Of health ; what makes the day and night —
  Some notion of astronomy ;

Treatment of neighbors at a feast —
  More genial ways of toasting them;
To love their fellow-men, at least
  A little, without roasting them.

No white sail found those coral bays,
  Wide rings of reefs defending them;
And so I lived my savage days,
  With little hope of ending them.
Three frightful years!   Though loved by some,
  A priest-led faction hated me,
Until it seemed that martyrdom,
  For all my pains, awaited me.

Fearful of change, and not content
  With foiling and defeating me,
My enemies once more were bent
  On finishing and eating me.
And so, not choosing to *assist*
  At their proposed festivities,
(All the more reason to resist
  Their cannibal proclivities!)

With scant provisions snatched in haste
  My small canoe encumbering,
Into the dim sea's rolling waste,
  While all the isle was slumbering,

One midnight, when the low late moon
    Across the shoals was shimmering,
I paddled from the still lagoon
    And channel darkly glimmering.

Five days adrift! the indolent
    Warm waves about me weltering:
The suns were fierce, my food was spent,
    And I was starved and sweltering:
When ho! a ship! How strange to meet
    Fair manners and urbanity!
How strange my native speech, how sweet
    The accents of humanity!

Thus all my efforts to redeem
    That sinister society
Were left behind, a nightmare dream
    Of horror and anxiety.
My changeful life was full and fleet;
    But long the hope attended me,
To see that land again, and greet
    The chiefs who once befriended me.

So, as I sailed those seas once more,
    When many years had passed away,
My ship dropped anchor off the shore
    Where I had been a castaway.

Amid the reefs we rowed to land,
   And, eager as a lover is
To seek his mistress, to the strand
   I strode, to make discoveries.

Less changed than my own life, appeared
   The wondrous island scenery;
Near by, the groves of cocoa reared
   Their fans of waving greenery;
There the old, shaggy, cane-thatched town;
   And, habited still sparingly,
The islanders came straggling down,
   And heard my questions staringly.

With signs of woe their arms they flung
   When I, in broken sentences
Of their well-nigh forgotten tongue,
   Inquired for old acquaintances.
"Dead! dead!" my friendly chiefs and they
   Who from the isle had driven me.
But when I spoke my sobriquet,
   The name the tribe had given me,

'Twas strange! the sudden eagerness
   And zeal with which they greeted it.
"Son-of-the-Great-Sea-Mother? yes!" —
   They joyfully repeated it.

" He's there ! "— They pointed. Bound to know
    What this amazing blunder meant.
Forthwith I followed to a low,
    Rude door, in utter wonderment.

Their temple! lined with sacred stones
    And heathen curiosities ;
Dried birds and fishes, reptiles' bones,
    And various monstrosities ;
Relics and charms, strung round the place,
    Trophies of fights and scrimmages ;
And, propped behind the central space.
    The rudest of carved images, —

Which I myself with shells and knife
    Had shaped, in my captivity !
A task to keep my heart and life
    From purposeless passivity.
The mouth too wide, too short the nose,
    How well I recollected it !
Now here, a grinning idol, those
    Sad wretches had erected it ;

Tricked and bedizened in a style
    Preposterous and laughable !
I gazed ; the guardian priest the while
    Eying me, grimly affable.

Swarthy and tall, with hideous smirk
   Admitting me to see it, he
Called it great magic, handiwork
   And image of their deity!

" Out of the ocean, in his sleep,"
   ('Twas hard to listen seriously!)
" He came to us, and in the deep
   Vanished again mysteriously.
He taught our people" (thus the priest's
   Narration is translatable)
" To discontinue at their feasts
   Some customs he found hatable;

" Not to hunt men, although we were,
   As now, a strong and bold people ;
Nor beat our women ; nor inter
   Alive our sick and old people :
To have more clothes and fewer wives.
   With houses more commodious ;
To speak true words, and make our lives
   In other ways less odious.

" These changes we found politic,
   Though backward in assuming them.
So now we leave our old and sick
   To starve, before inhuming them.

While yet some rich men on the coast
   Practice the old polygamy,
The poor have one wife, or, at most,
   Confine themselves to bigamy.

"And though some warriors of renown
   Continue anthropophagous,
'Tis rare that human flesh goes down
   The low caste man's œsophagus.
Woman we seldom beat, while she
   Is faithful and obedient;
We only hunt an enemy,
   And lie when it's expedient.

"Old men remember, still a few,
   How he appeared and talked with them;
Though not till he was gone they knew
   A deity had walked with them.
This image in his hands became
   The very form and face of him;
So now we call it by his name,
   And worship it in place of him;

"And in our sorceries draw from it
   Responses and admonishment."
All which I heard with infinite
   Misgiving and astonishment,

"THE CLUMSY IDOL FELL AT ONCE
AGAINST THE MUMMIES ON THE WALL." ETC

That fable thus should swallow fact,
   And truth to myth degenerate,
And I by wooden proxy act
   The god, for tribes to venerate!

I said, " The being you adore,
   Who came and went in mystery,
Was but a sailor washed ashore!"
   And told the simple history.
" My words and work your prophets foiled,
   They treated me despitefully,
And I escaped."   The priest recoiled,
   And glared upon me frightfully.

" And as for this dumb log " — I felt
   Such absolute disgust with it,
I twirled my walking-stick and dealt
   An inconsiderate thrust with it.
" Taboo! taboo!"   Too late the call:
   The clumsy idol fell at once
Against the mummies on the wall,
   The rattling skins and skeletons.

The priest, in horror at my speech,
   Had glared, aghast and stammering;
But now he raised his warning screech,
   And half the tribe came clamoring.

My comrades hurried me away,
    While, close behind us clattering,
The mob pursued us to the bay,
    And clubs and stones fell pattering.

Embarking, we in haste let fall
    The gifts which I had brought for them.
But more than this, alas for all
    My hopes! I could do naught for them ;
Nor could I venture more among
    The clans of that vicinity,
Because I had with impious tongue
    Denied my own divinity.

SENATOR GRANDILOW.

IF I were Senator Grandilow,
　　Mounting the marble portico,
Going to speak where Sumner spoke,
To waken the echoes Webster woke,
While the anxious nation waits to hear
Peals of warning or notes of cheer,
Wouldn't my pulse tingle and my heart glow, —
If I were Senator Grandilow?

I say to myself, when Grandilow
Looks smilingly down on friend and foe,
Thumb in waistcoat, quite at home
Under the flag-topped senate dome,
Fearless of front and valiant of lung,
With a nimble wit and a silvery tongue, —
" Ah, would some power on me bestow
The glorious gifts of a Grandilow!"

I gaze in wonder at Grandilow!
His eloquence bursts, a bright *jet d'eau.*
Diamond-crested, rainbow-spanned,
A pillar of light over all the land.

41

A beacon of hope to a people long
Groping in shadows of doubt and wrong;
At least I fancy it might be so,
If I were Senator Grandilow.

For, if I were Senator Grandilow,
A chosen chief, would I forego
The privilege of the hour and place,
To lead, enlighten, and lift my race ?
To rise sublime above private ends,
The clamors of faction, the claims of friends,
And strike for the right one downright blow, —
If I were a leader like Grandilow ?

Would I (suppose I were Grandilow,
Sachem of the mighty bow !)
Envenom my shafts with spleen and pique,
Make base alliance with ring and clique,
And mix with solemn affairs of state
Powwow of passion and party hate ?
Well, yes, I might, but would I, though,
If I were Senator Grandilow ?

I am not skilled, like Grandilow,
To graft my fortunes and make them grow
On flourishing boughs of the nation's tree;
I haven't the arts of such as he,

Prosperous patriots who have made
Their country's service a thriving trade;
Her needs their steps to rise by; — no,
I haven't the knack of a Grandilow.

Is it fitting (pardon me, Grandilow,
If the question seems malapropos)
That a favored son should bring to her
A thrice-divided love; prefer
To the public good his party's call,
Clan before party, and self before all?
Are there no debts, but the debts you owe
A certain Senator Grandilow?

For, let me say to you, Grandilow, —
Mounting the marble portico,
With your fist gripped full of the bolts of fate,
For a stand-up fight in the strifes of state, —
The horizon is larger than your hat,
The world is wider than your cravat,
A fact you possibly may not know; —
Think of it, will you, Grandilow?

No patent-reaper, O Grandilow,
Will reap a harvest we do not sow!
Error is violent, truth is strong;
The present is brief, the future long;

And History writes with an iron pen ;
Time wags his sifter of deeds and men,
And into it straightway we must go ;
Where then will be Senator Grandilow ?

Then take my advice, dear Grandilow !
Don't soar so high nor stoop so low ;
Quit your trained horses of craft and pride :
The world admires the way you ride,
But the world has other things to do
Than to watch the hoop while you jump through.
The Senate isn't a circus show,
Senator ! Senator Grandilow !

"WHEN WE CAME FROM THE WAR."

SONG OF THE POORHOUSE VETERANS.

OUR people, when first we came home from the
    war,
Before they forgot what the fighting was for,
Came out with gay bands, and a wonderful noise
Of cannon and shouting, to welcome us boys.
Our riddled old regiment marched in its rags
Under arches of triumph and billowy flags,
That made the poor shred of our ensign ashamed;
And orators under an awning declaimed;
And loud were the plaudits; and handkerchiefs
    waved
When they talked of the Union our armies had
    saved,
And vowed that our victories made up a debt
Which a bountiful nation would never forget,
    When first we came home from the war.

But the fervor of greeting died out with the sound
Of the guns and the trumpets, and some of us found

That with toil and exposure and wounds badly
    healed
We had left the best part of ourselves on the field;
While at home younger men had stepped into our
    place,
And put us old limpers quite out of the race.
Our welcome wore off, and the often-told tale
Of our services soon became hackneyed and stale.
Kind souls, when we offered small wares at their
    doors,
Would buy them in pity, but voted us bores,
And could hardly believe that the blue-coated tramps
Were ever acquainted with battles and camps,
    Or ever came home from the war.

At length they decided to settle us down
In the almshouse, with other poor wrecks of the
    town.
No parade of gay bands and great crowds thronging
    near
With flags and orations to welcome us here!
But the rosy-faced keeper received us, and said
That we ought to be thankful for shelter and bread.
Now, troubled no more with our needles and soap,
And the sight of gaunt men without health, without
    hope,

Who sadly remind them of services past,
Our kind-hearted people have leisure at last
To forget all about what the fighting was for,
And the promises made when we came from the war,
      When first we came home from the war.

THE KANSAS FARMER.

WE talked or read, or idly sat, beholding,
   Betwixt the wire-strung poles and April sky,
From dawn till dusk, the endlessly unfolding,
   Swift panorama of the land sweep by.

The twilight closed upon a lonesome prairie, —
   A paling sunset pierced by one faint star,
Above a house low-browed and solitary,
   Seen from the windows of our passing car.

For miles there was no other habitation.
   Out from a neighboring marsh a heron took flight,
Rose. gray and silent as an exhalation,
   And grew a speck far in the fading light.

Framed by the doorway in the frowning gable,
   The figure of a man stood dark and still;
No roof beside, but just a turf-walled stable,
   Half-thatched with grass, half-sunken in the hill.

A solemn mule couched on his bony haunches ;
  A lank sow leaned and rubbed against her sty ;
No tree, but one bare locust, in whose branches
  Turkeys were roosting, black against the sky.

The man stood gazing, gaunt of frame and gloomy ;
  So melancholy and so motionless,
A sharp compassionating thrill shot through me,
  With thinking of his utter loneliness.

Far from the cheerful light of human faces,
  The glow of friendly converse, how could he
Endure a lot as bare of all the graces
  As the surrounding hills of house or tree ?

He gazed as if with sad surmise and longing —
  As thick as sparks above the rushing train,
His kindled thoughts and aspirations thronging
    Toward some great good which he could never
      gain.

He saw each day that mighty, thundering shuttle
  Across the continent hurled to and fro ;
But of the life, the invisible and subtle
  Wide web it wove, how little could he know !

The train flew on, and, snugly housed within it,
 We saw the lonely exile left behind ;
But not till that brief vision of a minute
 Was photographed forever in the mind.

The train sped on with loud, relentless clanging ;
 But gentler fancies in my heart awoke,
As I recalled, in the wan twilight hanging
 Above his roof, a wreath of cottage smoke.

Symbol of household cheer the whole world over !
 Perfect contentment brims no mortal breast ;
The dweller with the prairie dog and gopher,
 No doubt, has his due portion with the rest.

His evening meal upon the coals was cooking ;
 A babe, I fain would think, made glad the house ;
A wife, I'm sure ; but he was anxious, looking
 To see his boys come driving home the cows.

No thought had he to join the world's great battle,
 Or follow in the ranks of wealth and pride.
His home, his farm, his own small herd of cattle,
 These are his world ; he knows no world beside.

Though few of life's fair consolations enter
   The door, to us so desolate and dim,
That cabin on the prairie is the center
   Of the round earth and rolling heavens to him.

He, too, — so fancy runs — has his ambition :
   To build a barn, renew that two years' loan,
Improve each day a little his condition,
   And leave his children's better than his own.

To petty cares, the lack of tools and fences,
   To rains, droughts, weeds, the price of pork and
      corn,
He gives his years ; yet finds its recompenses,
   Even in the life we picture so forlorn.

Man, to the last a child, who still amuses
   Himself all day with trifles great and small,
Cherishes most the few poor toys he uses,
   But, given too many, learns to scorn them all.

Sweeter than ease, sometimes. is rude privation ;
   Less tedious than long leisure to live through
Are days full packed with healthful occupation ;
   Too many friends, as irksome as too few.

How little for our daily need suffices,
　Could each but know, contented with his share!
The frugal dish, which luxury despises,
　Is to the humble sweet and wholesome fare.

With hope, a constant, cloud-illuming crescent,
　With love, and work for head or hands, these
　　　three,
Alike the mightiest king or lowliest peasant
　Finds life worth living, each in his degree.

Culture and gold are good, but not by building
　More stately porches may we look to win
Peace to our dwelling; nor by gayly gilding
　The fountain can we raise the flood within.

We ply the fount with toil and rest and revel,
　One casts in empires, and one bagatelles;
Still happiness in men will seek its level,
　As water from one source in many wells.

A MOTHER'S TRAGEDY.

HE fell in a wayside brawl, not far from his
           mother's door.
We picked him up, two or three of us; one ran on
           before,
To give her a decent warning, while we turned into
           the place,
Lugging him, horribly limp, with his hat laid over
           his face.

We heard a sharp voice in the doorway: "Don't fear
           but I shall be strong!
What is one sorrow the more to a heart that is seared
           with wrong?
My son? something dreadful? They've killed him!"
           And tearless, terrible eyes
Looked down on us and our burden: no wringing of
           hands, nor cries:

But, going before, she cleared the lounge that we laid
    him on ;
Uncovered with her own hand the face upstaring and
    wan,
The small, dark wound in the temple, and slow, dull
    trickling red ;
Then writhed in a spasm of horror and agony over
    the dead.

The doctors came and looked grave; there was
    nothing more to be done ;
And there the old mother sat by the side of her
    murdered son,
Rigid, erect, and under her neatly combed white
    hair
Her gleaming features fixed in a frozen and fierce
    despair.

The neighbors gathered round, where she sat tearless
    and grim ;
Full of compassion for her, but hardly sorry for
    him ;
Full of compassion for her, but wondering if, on the
    whole,
'Twere better to wish her joy, or weakly attempt to
    console.

She seemed to fathom their thoughts : " Yes, little
cause," she said.
" Did ever he give while living, that I should mourn
for him dead !
And life is so full of misfortunes that death seems
far from the worst.
Yet he is the babe of my bosom, the child I have
borne and nursed.

" The same ?   O, merciful powers !   'twas well that I
couldn't see
On the innocent forehead I kissed the horror that
was to be !
Not see these clotted locks in the silky hair I
curled —
The happiest mother and prettiest baby in all the
world.

" He sickened, too, that summer, just after his father
died ;
And well do I recollect how I clung to him then, and
cried.
And called on the cruel fates, and promised to
forgive
All their unkindness to me, if only my child might
live.

"'Spare him!' I said, 'whatever my widowed life
    must bear;
Spare him!' And the cruel fates, in mockery of
    my prayer —
Or was it Heaven, to punish my obduracy and
    pride? —
Seemed in mercy to grant what mercy would have
    denied.

" There are sons who honor their mothers; and is
    there an earthly joy
Like hers who watches the growth in grace of her
    one dear boy?
But look at us now, and tell me if ever I was
    one
That dreamt she was such a mother and he would be
    such a son!

" I bore with his childish passions, and petted his
    whims, until
They grew to be snarling faults of ingratitude and
    self-will.
I tried to curb and restrain them, but they were too
    fierce and strong,
And they turned and tore the hand that had fostered
    them too long.

" I hid in my heart, and pardoned, whatever wrong
    he had done ;
And strangers said : ' What a treasure you have in
    your only son ! '
And oh ! he was fair to behold !   And I marveled
    how he could be
Always so kind to others, and never kind to me.

" Upon those who gave him least, he could smile like
    an angel of light ;
Upon me, who gave him most, he vented his anger
    and spite.
Was it his, or mine, the fault ?   And whose, at last,
    was the blame,
When the fire in his blood broke out in open riot and
    shame ?

" He was as he was : perverse — a nature that under-
    stood
Nothing of self-denial, of duty or gratitude ;
No aim but the hour's enjoyment, no higher ambition
    on earth
Than just to be ranked good fellow with fellows of
    shallow worth.

" With a greed that had no eyes to see beyond the
    day,
Me and my slender savings he looked upon as his
    prey ;
In the sieve of self-indulgence pouring his powers
    and gains ;
Never counting the cost in future losses and pains.

" He was as he was : if your boy is born with a
    crippled limb,
Or blind, or deaf, do you think of laying the blame
    on him ?
And one is infirm of reason, and one is deformed of
    soul,
And one, a Goliath of passion, a pigmy in self-
    control.

" He was as he was, from his birth — no will or wish
    of his own ;
Or the will was flesh of his flesh, the wish was bone
    of his bone.
It is easy to say, we are free to follow evil or
    good ;
Whatever we follow or leave, the choice is in our
    blood.

"O, yes! he should have cared for good men's
    counsel and praise,
And heeded the pleading love that strove with him
    all his days.
But the force that obeys the magnet is not in stone,
    but in steel ;
And the secret is in ourselves of the influences we
    feel.

" He was as he was! He was born so! No need to
    question why
He was cursed with faults that neither his father had
    nor I.
Traits good in themselves sometimes appear in strange
    excess,
And generous heats flame out in folly and reckless-
    ness.

" You sooner might track the wind, or an under-
    ground stream to its source,
Than some inherited taint through its hidden and
    fitful course —
The vice that has lurked so long in generations
    past,
To burst its decent bounds and rage in our sons at
    last.

" He was as he was ; accuse him, excuse him, what
      you will :
And I, who have loved him most, and pitied, accuse
      him still.
For, though we may bear and forbear, and pardon,
      and suffer long,
The right is forever right, and the wrong is eternally
      wrong.

" And I am his mother ; and all that is left of my
      boy lies there !
The frolic of youth, and the frenzy, alternate sport
      and despair ;
Desire that would have dissolved — a mere lump in
      his cup — the earth !
Gone out like a flame that is quenched, like a fire
      that is dead on the hearth.

" I can neither rejoice nor grieve — my heart is like
      stone in my breast.
He was naught but a burden and thorn, and I know
      that what is, is best.
Yet I shall be lost without him.   The very trouble
      and care
That pass with him out of my life will leave it empty
      and bare.

"I would hope ; I would pray for him ! Is there
    another and happier sphere,
Where the soul may arise from the cloud of evil that
    clung to it here ?
Or has he rushed into that world all aflame with the
    passions of this ?
I would hope ; I would know ! I cannot look into
    the dark abyss !

" Maybe not all are immortal ; the souls of sinners
    may die,
Burn briefly in Heaven, and vanish, like meteors
    dropped in our sky.
I shall follow him soon, I shall follow ; and oh ! that
    our spirits may live,
If only to know each other, to know and embrace
    and forgive ! "

The neighbors gathered near, and departed, one by
    one ;
And there the old mother sat by the side of her
    murdered son,
And talked, and now and then brushed the flies from
    the livid face,
Till the coroner hurried in, and she rose to yield him
    place.

With a sob in her voice, she moved at last from the
    dead man's side,
A hard, dry sob from the source which grief long
    since had dried,
And still with the icy despair, the look out of eyes
    that had shed
So many tears for the living, they had none to weep
    for the dead.

AFTER THE SALE.

THE wagon, with high fantastic load
     Of household goods, is at the gate ;
The shadows darken down the road ;
     Why does the old man wait ?
Bureau, bedstead, rocking-chair,
Upturned table with heels in air, —
Whatever the grudging fates would spare, —
Lie huddled and heaped and tumbled there,
     A melancholy freight !

" Of all his riches," the teamster said,
     " Now only this precious pile remains !
A blanket and bed for his old gray head,
     For all his life-long pains.
Hard case, I own ! but they say that Pride
Must have a fall."   His ropes he tied
In the chill March wind.   " Hurry up ! " he cried,
     And gathered in the reins.

The old wife bows her stricken face
     On the doorstone, weary and worn and gray.

The old man lingers about the place,
    Taking a last survey;
Looks in once more at the great barn door,
On the empty mow and the vacant floor:
All the gains of his life have gone before,
    And why should he care to stay?

Only a stool with a broken leg
    Is left, and a bucket without a bail.
The harness is gone from hook and peg,
    Even the whip from its nail:
Dreary shadows hang from the wall.
No friendly whinny from shed or stall,
Nor unmilked heifer's welcoming call;
The poultry and pigs have vanished. all
    Swept out by the sheriff's sale.

Back to the dooryard well he goes
    For a parting look, a farewell drink.
How drippingly that bucket rose
    And poised for him on the brink,
In the summers gone, and plashed his feet.
When the men came in from the harvest heat!
How blessedly cool the draught, how sweet,
    'Tis misery now to think.

— " ALL
SWEPT OUT BY THE SHERIFF'S SALE."

What scenes of peaceful, prosperous life
    Once filled the yard, so desolate now!
When he often would say to his pleased, proud wife,
    That the farm appeared, somehow,
More thrifty and cheery than other men's,
With its cattle in pasture and swine in pens,
Bleating of lambs and cackle of hens,
    And well-stored crib and mow.

The early years of their proud success,
    The years of failure and mutual blame,
Are past, with the toil that was happiness,
    And the strife that was sorrow and shame.
She came to him hopeful and strong and fair —
Now who is the sad wraith sitting there,
With her burden of grief, and her old thin hair,
    Bowed over her feeble frame?

"Do you remember? This well," he said,
    "Was sunk that summer when Jane was born.
She used to stand in the old house-shed
    And blow the dinner-horn,
In after years, — or climb a rail
Of the dooryard fence for a cheery hail, —
Then run to the curb for a brimming pail,
    When I came up from the corn."

Why think of her now ? against whose name
    His lips and heart long since were sealed ;
Whose memory in their lives became
    A sorrow that never has healed.
Her step is on the creaking stair,
Her girlish image is everywhere !
He hears her laughter, he sees her hair
Blow back in the wind, as she comes to bear
    His luncheon to the field.

" 'Twas a terrible wrong !"   The old wife spoke,
    Swaying her gaunt frame to and fro.
" I'll say it now !"   Her strained voice broke
    Into a wail of woe.
" It haunts me awake, it haunts me asleep !
And silence has been so hard to keep —
So long ! — but there is a grief too deep
    For ever a man to know !"

A quaver of anguish shook his tone.
    His look was pierced with a keen remorse :
" The blame, I suppose, was all my own ;
    And I have no heart, of course !
Great Heaven ! nor any grief to hide !"
Lifting his gloomy hat aside,

He looked up, haggard and hollow-eyed,
Like one whose burning soul had dried
   His tears at their very source.

" No, no ! I don't mean that," she wept.
   " I've felt you suffering many a day,
And often at night when you thought I slept,
   And when I have heard you pray
Until it seemed that my heart would burst.
And as for the blame, you know, at first,
I claimed you were right, and did my worst
   To force her to obey,

"For the dream of our lives had been to make
   Our Jane a lady fit for a lord ;
Our schemes were all for our children's sake,
   And it seemed a cruel reward
To see her with careless scorn refuse —
For all the arguments we could use —
The men you most approved, and choose
   The one you most abhorred.

" But when she had chosen and all was done,
   You needn't have been so hard and stern
We might have forgiven the poor dear one,
   And welcomed her return.

You never could know what she was to me,
You never will know how I yearn to see
My child again — how homesickly
    I yearn, and yearn, and yearn!

" She chose for herself, and who can tell ?
    She braved your will, it's true, and yet
She may, for all that, have chosen well.
    And how can we forget?
We chose for Alice, and unawares
Rushed with her into a rich man's snares,
Who tangled us up in his loose affairs,
    And dragged us down with debt."

" Well, well ! " — with a heavy sigh — " Let's go !
    I haven't been always wise.   Ah, Jane !
Some things might not be done just so,
    If they were to do again.
But Alice is dead and the farm is gone ;
Our hopes, and all that we built them on,
Friends, wealth, are scattered hither and yon,
    And only ourselves remain.

" These boughs will blossom and fruits will fall
    The same !   When I changed the orchard lot,
And fenced it all with good stone wall,
    And planned the garden plot,

"AND NOW GOES FORTH BY AN OLD MAN'S SIDE,
A WEARY WANDERER."

And built the arbor and planted trees,
And made a home for our pride and ease,
We little thought these were all to please
    Strangers who knew us not!

"Others will reap where we have sown;
    But others never can understand
What watchful care these fields have known,
    Or how I loved the land.
Here maids will marry and babes be born,
The sun will shine on the wheat and corn,
Crops be gathered and sheep be shorn,
    But by a stranger's hand.

"Come, wife!" With bitterest vain regret,
    Remembering all good things that were,
The old man yet can half forget
    His woes, in pity of her.
She entered, a young man's happy bride,
She crowned his home with hope and pride,
And now goes forth by an old man's side,
    A weary wanderer.

With slow, disconsolate, broken talk,
    They look their last and pass the gate;
The wagon is gone and they must walk;
    A mile, and it's growing late.

She bears a parcel, he lifts a pack.
But what do they see there, up the track,
Against the sunset, looming black ?
'Tis strange ! the wagon is coming back
    With its melancholy freight.

And what is the driver shrieking out ?
    Now Heaven for a moment keep them sane !
" Turn about ! turn about ! " they hear him shout,
    As he flourishes whip and rein —
" You've a home and a good friend yet, you'll find ! "
A coach is following close behind ;
A face — a voice — O, Heaven be kind !
O, lips that tremble and tears that blind !
    O, breaking hearts, it's Jane !

THREE WORLDS.

I.

IN youth the world, a newly blown
    Prismatic bubble,
Shows the enchanted soul her own
    Enchanting double.

The light and dew of heavenly dreams
    Filled my young vision,
And life rose clothed in orient beams,
    Bright apparition !

Then love in each fair bosom beat,
    A pure emotion ;
And friendship was a long and sweet
    Ideal devotion.

Woman was truth ; and age was then
    Holy as hoary.
Strangely about the brows of men
    There shone a glory,

A radiance shed by my rapt sight
　　And reverent spirit ;
How changed the life, how paled the light,
　　As I drew near it !

'Twas my own ardent youth (alas,
　　How unsuspected !)
Whose image in the bubble's glass
　　I saw reflected.

O magic youth, that could suffuse
　　The bright creation
With its own dreams and rainbow hues
　　Of aspiration !

II.

The wondrous years no more were mine,
　　When fervent Fancy
Remade the world by her divine,
　　Sweet necromancy.

But still, as paled that earlier flame,
　　My zeal grew warmer
To serve my kind ; and I became
　　A world-reformer.

For every problem then I saw
    Some new solution,
Could I remodel human law
    And institution!

To wed in work the heart and mind,
    Make life a mission
Of wise good-will to all mankind,
    Was my ambition.

Bondage and ignorance should cease;
    Reason and culture
Should banish war, the dove of peace
    Succeed the vulture.

But patiently as I reshaped
    The old equation.
I found some factor still escaped
    My calculation.

No philosophic scheme, nor act
    Of legislature,
Can yoke the storm and cataract
    Of human nature.

The moral crusade may proceed
    By means immoral;
And too much zeal for peace may lead
    To many a quarrel.

A thankless task has he who tries
    To chip and model
The world to just the form and size
    Of his own noddle.

Is it because of hopes long tossed,
    Or heart grown harder?
Now I have also something lost
    Of that last ardor.

No dungeon door will cease to creak,
    Nor chain be broken,
For any word I hoped to speak,
    But leave unspoken.

My noon is past, as many things,
    Alas, remind me!
Slowly about my shadow swings,
    Lengthening behind me.

The unaccomplished task laid down
    I leave to others ;
The voice, the victory, and the crown,
    To you, my brothers !

Not doubting, though my lips be dumb,
    But trusting wholly
In that fair time which yet shall come,—
    Shall come, though slowly.

Not in our hurrying years, but late,
    Through generations,
The race shall rise which I await
    With perfect patience.

Youth's brave illusion, manhood's hope,
    Vision of sages,
Are augury and horoscope
    Of future ages.

A harp-like sound is in my ear,
    A far-off humming :
I see the golden cloud, I hear
    The chariots coming !

III.

Nearer and sweeter than I thought,
        One world has waited,
Though not the world my fancy wrought,
        Or hope created :

A world of common light and air,
        Of earth and azure ;
Of love girt round by fear, and care
        Dearer than pleasure ;

Of simple wants and few, good-will
        To friend and neighbor ;
And each day's cup each day must fill
        With thought and labor ;

Furtherance and help, with ample scope
        For tears and laughter ;
Of child-like faith, and earnest hope,
        In the hereafter ;

Patience in pain ; in every ill,
        Cross, and privation,
If not contentment, patience still,
        And resignation.

My brother's wrong I may not right,
 But I can share it ;
My own I'll study less to fight,
 And more to bear it.

The nettle-sting of others' deeds
 I'll strive to pardon,
And look to find the lurking weeds
 In my own garden.

I'll till my little plot of ground,
 And pay my taxes,
And let the headlong globe go round
 Upon its axis.

Aspire who may to seize the helm
 And guide creation,
If I can rule my little realm
 With moderation,—

My own small kingdom, act and thought
 And chaste affection,
Trained powers, and passions duly brought
 Into subjection,

The world of home, of wife and child,—
　　Good-by, ambition!
I'll live serenely reconciled
　　To my condition.

With years a richer life begins,
　　The spirit mellows:
Ripe age gives tone to violins,
　　Wine, and good fellows.

I'll marry action to repose,
　　Busily idle,
As through great scenes a traveler goes
　　With slackened bridle.

To loftier aims let me aspire,
　　To higher beauty;
Freedom to follow my desire
　　Be one with duty.

About our common mother earth
　　Flow seas of ether;
Heaven holds her in her starry girth,
　　The clouds enwreath her.

Forever mystery, love, the soul'
    Boundless ideal,
Like a diviner ether rolls
    About the real.

And second youth can still suffuse
    The bright creation
With its own dreams and rainbow hues
    Of aspiration.

THE SEEKING.

I.

BY ways of dreaming and doing,
　　Man seeks the bourn of the blest;
Youth yearns for the Fortunate Islands,
　　Age pines for the haven of rest.

And we say to ourselves, " Oh ! surely,
　　Beneath some bluer skies,
Just over our bleak horizon,
　　The land of our longing lies."

Each seeks some favored pathway,
　　Secure to him alone;
But every pathway thither
　　With broken hearts is strown.

II.

The Giver of Sleep breathed also,
　　Into our clay, the breath
And fire of unrest, to save us
　　From indolent life in death.

84

Fair is the opening rose-bud.
  And fair the full-blown rose;
And sweet, after rest, is action,
  And, after action, repose.

But indolence, like the cow-bird,
  That's hatched in an alien nest,
Crowds out the native virtues,
  And soon usurps the breast.

Better the endless endeavor,
  The strong deed rushing on,
And Happiness that, ere we know her
  And name her, smiles and is gone!

III.

We wait for the welling of waters
  That never pass the brink:
We pour our lives in the fountain,
  But cannot stay to drink.

" To-morrow," says Youthful Ardor,
  Twining the vine and the rose,
" I will couch in these braided bowers,
  As blithe as the breeze that blows."

" To-morrow," says earnest Manhood,
    Yet adding land to land,
" I will walk in the alleys of leisure,
    And rest from the work of my hand."

" To-morrow," says Age, still training
    The vine to the trembling wall,
Till the Dark sweeps down upon us,
    And the Shadow that swallows all.

IV.

Ebb-tide chased by the flood-tide,
    Night by the dawn pursued,
And ever contentment hounded
    By fresh inquietude !

Not what we have done avails us,
    But what we do and are ;
We turn from the deed that is setting,
    And steer for the rising star.

We may wreck our hearts in the voyage ;
    But never shall sail or oar,
Nor wind of enchantment, waft us
    Nearer the longed-for shore.

In vain each past attainment ;
   No sooner the port appears
Than the spirit, ever aspiring,
   Spreads sail for untried spheres.

Whatever region entices,
   Whatever siren sings,
Still onward beckons the phantom
   Of unaccomplished things.

HYMN OF THE AIR.

NOURISHER and encloser of all life
  Am I. Before man was, or beast, or tree,
I in my wingéd chariot moved upon
The desolate, weltering waste that was the world,
And bade it fructify. And life appeared :
Innumerable transitory forms
Limned and erased in each successive age,
Their early outlines lost, or later known
Traced in the rocky tablets of the globe.
Strange, wingless birds that tracked the baking
          sands ;
Ophidian and amphibian, and the huge
Iguanodon, and mighty beasts that tore
Tall forests, pasturing on their succulent boughs ;
These and their kind, emerging from the dim,
Slow-wakening, solitary, uncouth orb,
Stalked forth,— rude types of creatures yet to be ; —
Rock-gnawing lichens that forerun the feet
Of violets ; fungi watery and gross ;
Mosses that build and belt the corpulent bog ;
And tree-like ferns enormous from the moist

And steaming earth towered densely; them I fed
On carbon from my over-brimming cup,
Storing it in their veins for future man.

Nourisher and encloser of all life :
All things that creep or fly, and they that dwell
Within the dim inhabitable deep,
And herb and shrub, and all fair waving forms
Of verdure, but for my sustaining might,
My presence and sustaining might withdrawn,
Would fail in universal void : breath, flame,
And sense, and strength of foot, and power of flight.
The condor, circling high above his crags,
Circling securely in my azure realm,
Earthward with all his plumes would drop like lead.
And sound would cease, with voice of bird and beast ;
The cataract in its plunge would make no noise ;
The tumbling billow on the foamless beach
Would lapse in silence ; even the waves would sink,
And all the bright seas to a ghastly film
Subside and shrivel, heaved by ghosts of tides.
Nor cloud would be, nor ever morning red,
Nor rains, nor rivers, nor the blessed dew.

About the seas I flow, an ampler sea,
Diaphanous and shoreless ; earth my floor,

The mountain-chains my reefs ; my surface waves,
Ethereal, tumbling high beneath the stars,
More silvery soft than aught but light itself,
And beautiful, could finite eyes behold,
But only spirits behold, whose radiant forms
Bathe in my almost spiritual flood.
Stupendous tides, to whose huge volume those
That ridge the broad-backed sea with sweeping
        swells
Are but as ripples, roll beneath the moon
Eternally, unchafed by any strand,
In unimaginable loneliness,
And silence broken by no sound save where
With fiery plash the raining meteors fall.

Far down, curved duly with the curving sphere,
The white clouds curdle, pierced by quiet crags ;
With rifts that show the large plan of the world,
Oceans and continents and ice-capped poles,
Rivers and towns and crawling beasts and men.
Forever, high above those realms of change,
I take the sunshine on my crest, and bare
My pure, cold bosom to the moon and stars ;
While at my feet the pictured seasons pass
In beauty, or amidst battling elements,

When clouds charge clouds and lightnings cross
    their swords,
And my wild skirts are fringed with flying storms.

I am the fountain of all winds that blow ;
Parent of zephyrs and flower-scented gales,
Sweet as the breath of lovers when they kiss
Under vine-shadows on soft summer eves.

Ministers of a vast beneficence,
Forever on fleet errands to and fro
My breezes fly ; beneath their glancing wings
Making the glad waves leap and clap their hands ;
Wafting through sun and shadow round the curve
Innumerable fleets ; fanning parched climes,
And purifying over-peopled towns ;
Bearing in airy urns to thirsty lands
The copious exhalations of the sea,
To frozen realms the heat of torrid suns.

Yet trust me not, for I am changeable :
Oh ! trust me not, for in my glassiest calms
Terror and fury couch, and tempest breeds.

My blue-roofed cavern is the nursing-place
Of rains and snows and hurricanes, the lair
Of young tornadoes and the whirlwind's whelps.

I am invisible, yet terrible.
All moods are mine.   The fleets I waft, I smite.
In their mad whirling dance my dread cyclones,
Turbaned with thunder-clouds, in roaring robes
Gathering the torn-up seas and desert sands,
Darken and devastate the affrighted globe.

Eternal battle-field of cold and heat;
Forever-swaying balance, reservoir
Of indestructible tumultuous force;
Wafter of ships; mother of fierce monsoons;
Dispenser of the heavenly rain and dew;
Purger of lands, physician of sick climes;
Floating in peace the rosy evening cloud,
Or curled white cirrus of midsummer noons;
Gentle or stern, in calm or tempest, I
Fulfill my manifold appointed use.

In my divine alembic I transmute
Death and the poisonous vapors of the world
Into fresh life and beauty.   Tribes of men,

Interminable processions, insect, brute,
The multitudinous tranquil race of plants.
All things that perish, in my chemic glass
Distill and change, exhale and disappear ;
The beauteous flower, and she more beautiful
Who lifts it from the stalk with loving hand ;
Tyrants and slaves, the eagle and the gnat,
Leviathan and python, lion and lamb :
I waste and mingle, I diffuse and blow
About the world their wandering elements,
To pour them forth anew in living forms.

Enfolder and disposer of all life
Am I : and yet not I : Oh ! faithless man,
How canst thou feel my power and mystery,
And know the invisible force that clasps thee round,
And have in me thy being, and yet doubt
The Spirit whose similitude I am,
The Power that framed the world, and me, and thee ?

THE POET.

A YOUTH there was, and his dwelling amid
great wonders stood;
There laughed the verdurous valley, there gloomed
the serious wood;
And round about were the voices of winds and of
rushing streams;
And his days were drugged with illusions, his nights
were drunken with dreams.

The years flew by, like the wild fowl, one by one,
over the glen,
Till a man he was grown, gazed after by men and
the daughters of men;
A bard in the midst of a people that trafficked and
schemed and wrought,
They red with the sunlight of action, he pale with
the moonlight of thought.

And many looked after and loved him, but wayward
    and rapt went he;
And blessed were his days, but ever he longed for
    better to be;
And fair and sweet were the maidens, but only the
    face of the gray,
Thin wraith, the bodiless moonshine, beside his
    pillow lay.

The strings of his lute never trembled to human
    joys and woes,
But told of the clouds and the flowers, and the love
    that no man knows:
He turned his song, as a Claude-glass, to image the
    shapes and gleams
That float in the Limbus of fancy, that drift in the
    Hades of dreams.

But once and again to his bedside a Vision of
    visions had come,
When the world was mantled in darkness, and all
    its voices were dumb,
Save only, afar in the forest, a moan and a glimmer
    of locks,
Where the lost brook wailed as it wandered, and
    beat its white breast on the rocks.

Then the chill dim space of his chamber unfolded
and bloomed as a flower,

Filling with glory and fragrance the lonely and
desolate hour;

Over his closed cold eyelids a breath moved, vital
and warm,

And a soul came out of the fragrance, and out of
the glory a form.

And in the still air of the heaven they made all
around and above,

Were eyes of ravishing brightness, a face of ineffable
love;

From a forehead of snow flamed backward the
hair's soft golden fire;

And a voice, or the soul of a voice, said, "I am your
heart's desire.

"Into life by the love of the sculptor a marble
maiden was warmed;

And out of your wish I was fashioned, and out of
your faith I was formed.

The word I utter is only a pearl of your innermost
thought;

My wisdom, the deep-hidden treasure that up from
your breast I have brought.

I am twin-born of your being : to every mortal is
    given
His angel, unseen, bending near him, as Earth is
    leaned over by Heaven ;
Both one, as the stem and the flower of the water-
    lily are one,
Below in the ooze and the shimmer, above in the
    azure and sun.

" I dwell in the life of the spirit, yet ever am close
    at your side ;
And I say to you, out of the stillness of light
    wherein I abide,—
O man ! in the midst of illusions, be ever alert to
    hear
The lisp of your Psyche, the whisper that breathes
    in the ear of your ear.

" O poet ! with doubt and denial vex not your mind
    overmuch :
They dull the delicate forces, the chords that
    respond to my touch.
The bounds of your metaphysics inclose but a sterile
    clod :
Waste not your thought upon thinking, nor dogma-
    tize about God.

" And dwell no longer in dreamland, the realm of
 fable and fay ;
Await not the feast of To-morrow, but break the
 bread of To-day.
Pine not for the nymph, Perfection, nor follow the
 glance of Pride ;
But beckon the helpful maiden, call Comfort to your
 side.

" Embody your pale ideals, and give to the dream
 of youth,
With the form of art, which is beauty, the soul of
 art, which is truth.
Fused in the fires of passion, in the fervor of fancy
 wrought,
In reason's ice-brook temper the flaming sword of
 your thought.

" Seize traits of the living and human,— no copy of
 copy and cast !
Nor swaddle the child of the Present in language
 and lore of the Past.
Find love in hearts that are nighest, contentment in
 common things,
And give to the creeping moment the lightness and
 splendor of wings.

Above the roofs of the lowly let Poesy hover and
    glance,
And set by the humblest highway the finger-post of
    Romance ;
Strong in the wisdom that counsels, and glad with
    the faith that consoles,
To guide men ever upward to higher and nobler
    goals ;

" To cheer with chants of the morning, or soothe
    with songs in the night ;
So live, a beguiler of sorrows and minister of
    delight !
And still, in the midst of illusions, be ever alert to
    hear
The word of your Psyche, the whisper that breathes
    in the ear of your ear.

" The angels are still descending that to the
    patriarch came ;
Just over each upturned forehead plays the celestial
    flame.
Above your doubts and repinings, the heavens are
    opened wide
To flood your life with the fullness of light wherein
    I abide.

" Within the trembling dew-drop, that toward the
      morning turns,
The world in little is mirrored, a whole creation
      burns ;
And every heart that is lifted, and every soul that
      aspires,
Is a spark of the Infinite Spirit, a focus of heavenly
      fires."

The vision departed, and over the world's dim
      boundary rolled
The shining billow of daybreak, the surges of
      crimson and gold.
The wheels of traffic resounded, the blows of the
      builders rang,
Sweet maidens smiled in the doorways, and children
      shouted and sang.

The cry of the sibilant saw-mill rose vehement and
      loud,
The white mill-waters curdled, and fell like a falling
      cloud ;
While afar on the misty lowland went flying the
      iron steed,
White-plumed, a phantom of beauty, swift-wheeled,
      a marvel of speed!

The Poet went forth, beholding the earth created
    new ;
He bathed his brow in its freshness, he washed his
    heart in its dew ;
He heard the chorus of farmyards, the jubilee of
    the birds,
The far-away tinkle, the lowing of pasture-going
    herds.

He saw the lake all a-shiver with pictures of shores
    and trees,
Soft etchings of cloud and shadow, the mezzotint of
    the breeze ;
And thinly ascending and curling, in clefts of the
    dark-green hills,
The smokes of embowered dwellings, like upward-
    winding rills.

He heard blithe sounds of labor blend with the
    brooks that ran,
The mighty rhythm of nature rhyme in the works
    of man ;
And whether he roamed the woodland, or traversed
    the busy street,
He moved in a world of wonders, with miracles at
    his feet.

And he vowed, " I will rend as a garment the dream
      I have dreamed so long,
Put living men in my measures, this light and this
      land in my song ;
For never was fabled country so fair as this I
      behold :
I dwell in a realm of enchantment, I live in an age
      of gold ! "

AT MOUNT DESERT.

BAR HARBOR.

In this rhyme of Mount Desert the more common pronunciation of the name is adopted, with the anomalous accent on the final syllable, which appears to be a survival from the French, not very desirable; while it is to be regretted that the full significance of the name given by the Voyageur Champlain to this " Island of the Desolate Mountains " — *Isle des Monts Deserts* — could not have been preserved.

The bird which flits through the ninth stanza is the black guillemot, a Northern waterfowl, bearing sufficient resemblance to a pigeon to suggest its local name; its nearly black plumage has a greenish tinge, with a conspicuous white spot on the wing. Its soft, plaintive whistle faintly suggests the note of the wood pewee. It frequents in great numbers some of the islands and crags of the far coast of Maine, where it breeds.

The harebell is scattered profusely almost everywhere along the shaded cliffs; its clusters are especially abundant and beautiful about Sol's Cliff, a ruggedly picturesque crag not far from Bar Harbor.

PANOPLIED with crags and trees,
        And begirt
By blue islands in soft seas,
        Which invert
Idle yachts on glassy days,—
Who shall paint your purple bays,
Who can frame you in a phrase,
        Mount Desert ?

103

Beetling ledges and sublime
     Ocean swells ;
Caverns green with weeds and slime,
     Blue with shells ;
Isle of rest for weary lives,
Woodland walks and dusty drives,
Seaside villas and big hives
     Of hotels.

Rocks where dreamers half the day
     Sit inert ;
Where girls gossip and crochet,
Play lawn-tennis, and, they say,
     Sometimes flirt ;
Place to read, or sketch, or row ;
Town of hops and shops and show :
By these tokens tourists know
     Mount Desert.

Every morning sees a mile,
     Less or more,
Of strange vehicles defile
     By your door :
Choose one, mount, and bowl along
On a buckboard light and strong,
Lilting, tilting on its long
     Limber floor.

Or the dismal fog shuts down,
    Chill and gray ;
Over harbor, coast and town,
Dismal, drizzling, it sweeps down,
    Day by day,
In interminable drifts,
Till some morning, lo, it lifts !
And again through ragged rifts
    Gleams the bay.

Sheeny vapors ride the air
    And the sea,
Touching, trailing, here and there,
Till each mountain seems to wear
    A toupee ;
Or a scimiter of lace
Shears a headland from its base,
And leaves hanging there in space
    Rock and tree.

Quit the world of news and dress,
    Cards and calls !
To the vaulted wilderness,
    Which inwalls
Mossy chasms and tangled nooks !

Where the fleeing wood-nymph looks
From the veils of flashing brooks
　　And swift falls.

Loose your snowy-pinioned skiff,
　　Launch in space !
Or explore with me this cliff,
　　From its face,
Which the wind and surges fret,
Past the plumèd parapet,
Where no touch of man has yet
　　Left a trace.

As you scale the splintered jag
　　Toward the sky, —
As you pass the jutting jag,
The sea-pigeons on the crag
　　Downward fly ;
From the swells not far remote,
Where the pied flock sits afloat,
Comes their softly whistled note,
　　Like a sigh.

Slim against the fringy line
　　Of the firs,
The outleaning birches shine ;

There the tresses of the pine;
  The wind stirs
The green-tufted tamarack;
And the cedars, bristling black,
In the mountain's craggy back
  Strike their spurs.

You may search the woods in vain,
  Everywhere,
For the lonely thrush, whose strain
  Fills the air.
Here the shy bunchberries house,
Where blue-tinted balsam boughs
Weave a covert for the grouse
  And the hare.

The white-throated sparrow sings
  In the trees.
Tint of mosses, glint of wings,
O, the thousand lovely things
  That one sees!
Loveliest, frailest, of them all
Are these wild flowers, blue and small,
Wavering on the bleak sea-wall
  In the breeze.

Find a foothold in the ledge,
    There they spring;
On its utmost dizzy edge,
    There they cling;
Where there's room for tuft to grow
In the crevices below,
While waves dash and tempests blow,
    There they swing!

Little Ariels that perform
    Their pure part
In rude scenes of strife and storm,
    They upstart
From gray cleft and scanty mould.
So late flowers of love unfold,
Sweet relentings, in some old,
    Rugged heart.

Region where the harebell blows,
    Wave-begirt!
Let the season's round of shows,
    Which divert
Careless eyes in yonder town,
Justify your fair renown;
But these flowers shall be your crown,
    Mount Desert!

By what magic, out of air,
        Do they spin,—
Out of sunlight, dew and air,
The slight bonnets that they wear,
        Blue and thin ?
Children of the rock and sky !
Little people, you and I
Surely by some mystic tie
        Are akin.

Huddled here in pleasant flocks
        On the verge,
Nodding hoods and fluttering locks,
Half-way down the rifted rocks
        That emerge
From the billows tumbling white,
Do you feel a fine delight
In the breezes and the bright
        Bursting surge ?

Larger cousins of these meek,
        Tiny elves !
Belles of Mount Desert, who seek
Your sweet namesakes on the bleak
        Crannied shelves ;
Following far the lovely lures,—

Dainty relatives of yours,
Little charming miniatures
　　　Of yourselves! —

Cull them here betwixt the brink
　　　And the foam!
Choose a cluster by the brink,
Lift them gently from their chink,
　　　Bear them home,—
Every flower a fairy vase
Brimmed with light of breezy bays,
In each bell the summer day's
　　　Azure dome!

To the city's footworn flags
　　　They will bring
Winds and voices of these crags,
　　　Where they cling,
Leaping surf and leaning trees,
Cool, bright hours of joyous ease,
And green islands in the sea's
　　　Shining ring.

THE BELL–BUOY AT MOUNT DESERT.

AT the gateway of the bay,
  On the currents that come and go,
The bell-buoy heaves and swings.
Forever seeming to say :
" Woe ! woe ! " to the mariner, " woe !
  Beware of the reefs below ! "
  To and fro, to and fro,
    The bell-buoy rocks and rings.

In calm or storm, through all
  The changes of night and day,
  Blithe sun or blinding spray,
    With the wail of the winds that blow,
    With the moan of the ebb and flow,
While the billows swell and fall,
Goes forth that warning call —
  Night and day, night and day,

111

Peals forth the mournful knell
Of that iron sentinel,
Of the wave-swung, warning bell,
  At the gateway of the bay.

Where the granite-snouted ledges
  Lurk in their pimpled hides,
    Scraggy with whelks and bosses,
    And shaggy with black sea-mosses,
Just showing the tawny edges
  Of their backs in the burying tides,
Shouldering off the foam ;
    Where they lie in wait to gore
  With their terrible tusks the sides
Of the fair ship flying home ;
  There the bowing bell-buoy rides,
    With a dull reverberant roar
    Evermore, evermore
Crying : " Woe ! " to the mariner, " woe !
Beware of the rocks below !
    Beware of the treacherous shore ! "

At evening, from your boat,
  You may see the sombre bell
    In its black and massy frame,
    Peered through by the sunset flame ;
A solemn silhouette,

In a skeleton turret, set
On the balanced and anchored float,
  A-swing with the crimson swell.

When the soft, slumberous haze
Of drowsy midsummer days
Pours around inlets and bays
  A glassy ethereal gleam ;
And over far isles and sails
Drop violet veils beyond veils,
  Till headland and cliff but seem
  The unreal shapes of a dream ;
When hardly the loon and gull,
In the lap of the languid lull,
  Appear to waver and dip :
Then the buoy sways, heavy and slow,
And the bell tolls, sad and low,
  Like the bell of a sunken ship,
That heaves with the heaving hull,
Wave-rocked on the reefs below.

At times to the dreamy eye,
  In the glamour of glistening weather
That girdles the sea and sky,
While ocean and island lie
  Like a lion and lamb together ;
When the billow that bursts its sheaf

Of silver over the reef
  Falls light and white as a feather,
Curled all the length of the reef;
Then the bell, like a darker plume,
Nods over the downy spume
  In the veiled voluptuous weather.

At times so gently stirred,
  It seems like a waving bough
To invite the wandering bird.
At intervals still is heard
  That sullen note — as now ! —
Clanging its mournful and lone
Perpetual monotone.

A dismal, dolorous sound,
  You would say, heard anywhere,
  Be the weather foul or fair !
Not so to the homeward-bound
Late crew from the fishing-ground,
  Some muffled and murky night;
Or the steamer heaving her lead
And groping in doubt and dread,
  Through drizzle and fog, by the light
Of her lantern eyes, which shed
A misty glare at her head;
  Reaching out quivering rays,

"A DISMAL, DOLOROUS SOUND."

Antennæ-like, in the haze,
To find her dubious way.
  To the pilot's practiced ear
    In such dark and anxious times,
That peal, as I have heard say,
  Signaling, sudden and clear,
  The course which he shall steer,
  Is a cheerier sound to hear
    Than sweetest belfry chimes.

But when, on this border-realm
  Of created things, once more
  The powers of chaos outpour
Their legions, and overwhelm
  With darkness and dire uproar,
  In their mad foray, this fair
  Frontier of created things;
When they scatter the fishing-fleet
And stun the shore with the beat
  And buffet of billowy wings,
And trample of thunderous feet —
What life, out there in the surges,
  Flings frantic arms in air
As it tosses and sinks and emerges —
  Beckons with wild despair,
    And tongues that doleful peal?

Now loud in the leaping surges,
   Now stifled with wind and wave.
No simple device of good
Stout metal and bolted wood,
     But surely a thing that can feel,
    And strong in its struggle to save
     The shoreward driving keel!
Boom! boom! boom!
Out of the horror of gloom
A sound of dolor and doom
     To the helmsman at the wheel.

The seasons come and go,
   And still in storm or calm,
    On the ocean's palpitant palm,
     The bell-buoy rocks and rolls.
The summers come and go,
And, mantled in whirling snow,
Ice-capped, amid foam and floe,
     The bell-buoy tumbles and tolls.
To and fro, loud or low,
   Ever that sound of fear!
   You listen and seem to hear
   A voice, as of some wild seer,
     A cry and a warning to souls
    Over life's treacherous shoals.

THE CABIN.

Read at the Claflin Garden Party given to Mrs. H. B. Stowe, in Celebration of her
Seventieth Birthday, June 14, 1882.

GENIUS, 'tis said, knows not itself,
    But works unconscious wholly.
Even so she wrought, who built in thought
    The Cabin of the Lowly.

A wife with common wifely cares,
    What mighty dreams enwrapt her!
What fancies burned, until she turned
    To write some flaming chapter!

Her life was like some quiet bridge,
    Impetuous tides sweep under.
So week by week the story grew,
    From wonder on to wonder.

Wisdom could not conceive the plot,
    Nor wit and fancy spin it;
The woman's part, the wife's deep heart,
    All mother's love, were in it.

Hatred of tyranny and wrong,
  Compassion sweet and holy,
Sorrow and Guilt and Terror built
  That Cabin of the Lowly.

And in the morning light, behold,
  By some divine mutation,
Its roof became a sky of flame,
  A portent to the nation!

The Slave went forth through all the earth,
  He preached to priest and rabbin;
He spoke all tongues; in every land
  Opened that lowly Cabin.

Anon a school for kinder rule,
  For freer thoughts and manners;
Then from its door what armies pour
  With bayonets and banners!

More potent still than fires that kill,
  Or logic that convinces,
The tale she told to high and low,
  To peasants and to princes.

That tale belongs with Freedom's songs,
  The hero's high endeavor,
And all brave deeds that serve the needs
  Of Liberty forever!

l greet her now, when South and North
  Have ceased their deadly quarrels;
And say, or sing, while here I fling
  This leaf upon her laurels: —

She loosed the rivets of the slave;
  She likewise lifted woman,
And proved her right to share with man
  All labors pure and human.

Women, they say, must yield, obey,
  Rear children, dance cotillons:
While this one wrote, she cast the vote
  Of unenfranchised millions!

ODE.

Read at the Dedication of the Soldiers' Monument at Arlington, Mass., June 17, 1887.

L IKE Peace itself, as calm and fair, —
    White flower from battle-furrows grown,
  Its beauty blossomed into stone, —
Stands this still shaft in this June air!

Long may the heavens upon it shed
  The dews of eve, the beams of morn,
  And light, for ages yet unborn,
The deeds of our heroic dead!

They kept their country's faith, and fought
  The New World's promise to fulfill, —
  To hold, and leave unbroken still,
The ring of States the fathers wrought.

As cheerfully each artisan,
  In some great work, performs his part,
  Though knowing not the Master's art
And purpose, in the perfect plan; —

122

So they, alike the sires and sons,
   Toiled at one pattern, one divine,
   Inscrutable and vast design,
Which through a nation's fabric runs.

They strove, at duty's high behest,
   For liberty and equal laws ;
   And in so striving served a cause
Whose grander scope they dimly guessed.

We ask not of their birth, nor need
   The story of their years be sung ;
   Who die for truth are always young,
And dear in their immortal deed.

Life at the best is brief, and wrong
   Is evermore to face and quell ;
   They who have done their duty well,
They only, have lived well and long.

Oh ! blessed are they whose troubled days
   Are nobly rounded, to our eyes,
   By some large act of sacrifice,
Beyond all earthly blame or praise.

No more shall cold detraction come
  To search their lives, nor fortune fret;
  The book is closed, and on it set
The sacred seal of martyrdom.

Friends, living comrades, gather round!
  And wave, ye winds, oh! gently wave
  The flag they loved and died to save,
Above our consecrated ground.

To them this fair memorial stone
  We raise, to be henceforth a sign
  Of patriot's zeal, and Freedom's shrine;
And Fame adopts them for her own.

AFTER THE CONCERT.

JOSEF HOFMANN, PIANIST AND COMPOSER, AGED 10.

THE tempest of applause he met
    As meekly as a bending bud!
A boy of humble birth, and yet
    A prince of more than royal blood.

For him no bauble handed down,
    No sceptre despot ever bore,
But Music's heavenly realm, the crown
    Which youthful Haendel won and wore!

How laughed the *Allegro's* gay disdain, —
    What rippling pearly melodies
Showered on us their enchanted rain, —
    When his small fingers swept the keys!

They leaped, they flew, they flashed through all
    The jubilant chords; or dropped, in play,
As carelessly as petals fall
    From cherry-boughs in breezy May.

He tossed us Schumann's sparkling airs ;
    Struck Rubinstein's sweet storms of tone :
We followed, up the starry stairs,
    The shining feet of Mendelssohn.

He wove, around an untried theme,
    So varied and so blithe a strain,
It wrapped us in a radiant dream
    Of little Wolfgang come again.

The very roof with plaudits shook ;
    And still, above their bursting flood,
The thunder and the gusts he took
    As simply as a swaying bud.

Ah, could he know, the wondrous boy!
    When he had vanished from our gaze,
What tearful yearnings veiled our joy,
    What prayers were mingled with our praise !

We longed to shield him from the gales
    Of coming time ; to lay his head
In lulling arms, and tell him tales,
    And fold him in his quiet bed.

Waste not too soon, O burning star!
   Your bright young life ; but nurse its beam,
That it may rise and light afar
   The world's unresting, troubled stream.

Heaven fend, from that too ardent heart,
   The griefs of great and gifted men,
The sordid miseries of Mozart,
   The woes of mighty Beethoven.

Heir to a throne unstained by wrong,
   Possess your sphere, unvexed by strife ;
Conquer new realms, rule well and long,
   Nor lose the deeper things of life.

The unsullied ray that guides the soul
   Is more than glory's blinding flame ;
And helpful manhood, sound and whole,
   Than all the works of art and fame.
January, 1888.

QUATRAINS AND EPIGRAMS.

ABRAHAM LINCOLN.

HEROIC soul, in homely garb half hid,
   Sincere, sagacious, melancholy, quaint,
What he endured, no less than what he did,
   Has reared his monument and crowned him saint.

TEMPTATION.

How sweet, till past, then hideous evermore!
   Like that false fay the legend tells us of,
That seemed a lovely woman, viewed before,
   But, from behind, all hollow, like a trough.

PHAETON.

HOT youth, in haste your high career to run,
Heed the wise counsel Phœbus gave his son,
And spare the whip! brace the firm reins with nerve,
Nor ever from the middle pathway swerve.

MATERIALIST.

He took a tawny handful from the strand :
" What we can grasp," he said, " we understand,
And nothing more : " when, lo ! the laughing sand
Slid swiftly from his vainly clutching hand.

IDEALIST.

The World is but a frozen kind of gas,
A transient ice we sport on, where, alas !
Diverted by the pictures in the glass,
We heed not the Realities that pass.

SENSUALIST.

" Live while we live ! " he cried ; but did not guess,
Fooled by the phantom, Pleasure, how much less
Enjoyment runs in rivers of excess
Than overbrims divine abstemiousness.

YEARS AND ART.

Youth strikes a skill-less blow, but the metal is all
    aglow ;
Age has the experienced hand, but the fire in the
    forge is low.

.

HOW CAN I WELCOME AGE?

How can I welcome age, or behold without dismay
The beautiful days go by and the great years glide
    away?
Lightly I hold the world, but I look upon children
    and wife,
And though I dread not death, they make me in
    love with life.

A POET-CRITIC.

HE writes anonymous reviews;
    The reason is well known :
To see in print some sure abuse
Of every rival poet's muse,
    And praises of his own.

AN ODIOUS COMPARISON.

WHEN to my haughty spirit I rehearse
    My verse,
Faulty enough it seems; yet sometimes when
I measure it by that of other men,
    Why, then —
I see how easily it might be worse.

DIDACTIC POET.

Poet! you do your genius wrong
　　By always reaching
For some deep lesson, spoil your song
　　By too much teaching.

Let brighter beauty, rising love,
　　Just hint your moral,
As whitening surges break above
　　The reef of coral.

THE REASON WHY.

Your thronged bright parlors are a paradise
I too would enter; but before my eyes
The doubting angel waves his two-edged sword —
The dread of boring and of being bored.

AN INDISCREET FRIEND.

Lucius defends me from my foes,
　　But wins no thanks from me:
Better a whole brigade of those
　　Than one such friend as he!

XAVIER DE MAISTRE'S EPITAPH ON HIMSELF.

(*From the French.*)

HERE lies, beneath this cold gray stone,
  Xavier, whom all things filled with wonder;
Who sought to know whence the winds blow,
  And how and why Jove rolls the thunder.

He many a book of magic prized,
  And read from morn till evening's fall,
And drank death's wave at last, surprised
  That he knew nothing after all!

ALCOTT.

(*Inviting a Friend to one of the early "Conversations."*)

Do you care to meet Alcott?   His mind is a mirror,
Reflecting the unspoken thought of his hearer:
To the great he is great, to the fool he's a fool:
In the world's dreary desert a crystalline pool.
Where a lion looks in and a lion appears;
But an ass will see only his own ass's ears.

BON VOYAGE!

(For the Farewell Banquet to F. H. U., before his departure for Glasgow.)

WHEN to the land of Scott and Burns,
    Bannocks and haggis, classic dishes!
Our friend departs, he takes our hearts
    Along with him, in all good wishes.

May these attend, a viewless throng,
    To guard the ship that bears him over!
No fog delay, nor storm, but may
    Kind fortune be his constant lover.

If tempests smite the wild seas white,
    And Titan billows reel and totter,
Let never plank go down with Frank,
    Nor Underwood be under water!

WIDOW BROWN'S CHRISTMAS.

HIS window is over the factory flume ;
　　And Elkanah there, in his counting-room,
　　　　Sits hugging a littered table.
His beard is white as the foam, and his cheek
Is weather-beaten and withered and bleak
　　　　As the old brown factory gable.

Christmas is near ; and he, it is clear,
Is squaring accounts with the parting year ;
Setting forth, in column and row,
Whatever a penny of gain can show —
Mortgages, dividends, and rents,
City bonds and gover'ments ;
A factory here and a tannery there.
Good bank stock and railroad share ; —
As fast as his busy brain can count.
　　　　Or his busy pen indite 'em.
Figuring profit and gross amount.
　　　　And adding item to item.

"SETTING FORTH IN COLUMN AND ROW,
WHATEVER A PENNY OF GAIN CAN SHOW."

Thinks he : " It's a good round sum I make ;
Don't seem much like I was goin' to break ! "
   And he looked again as he poised his pen
      To fillip the drop of ink off.
But just as he gave the pen a shake,
He said " Ho ! ho ! " at a strange mistake
      He found himself on the brink of :
He said "Ha ! ha ! " and his lips drew in
With a hard, dry, leathery kind of grin,
   As much like the smile of a crocodile
      As anything you can think of.

" I declare ! there's Widder Brown
In the cottage over in Tannery Town !
The family had the house rent free
As long as her husband worked for me.
A good, smart, faithful chap was Jim —
Wish I had forty as good as him !
But he died one day, and left her there ;
And I put the place in the parson's care —
For the only man in the town I dare
      To trust is Parson Emery,
To see that the house don't run away,
And collect the rent she agreed to pay.
I'll write a letter this very day,
      To jog the good man's memory."

The letter was straightway penned and sent;
And it preached hard times to a dreary extent:
" For money is tight at ten per cent;
Often no sooner got than spent;
The poor man finds it a heavy stent
    To earn his mess of pottage;
And so," concluded the argument,
" You may, if you please, remit the rent
    Jim's widder owes for the cottage."

In two days' time the answer came.
" The parson is prompt.   But — what in the name!"
He cried, as he opened and read the same:
    How extremely odd it sounded!
" Dear, noble, generous, honored friend " —
Were terms he couldn't well comprehend;
And when he had struggled on to the end,
    He was utterly astounded.

He gasped and gurgled, and then burst out:
" What'n thunder's the ol' fool ravin' about?
He's crazy, without a shadder o' doubt!
A-writin' to me as if I was a saint!
Wa'al, mabby I be, and then mabby I ain't.
An' what's his argyment? why, to be sure,
That I'm a marciful man to the poor,

An' feel for the sufferin' brother,
An' stay the widder whose staff is gone;
An' so he continners a-layin' it on,
 An' he ain't sarcastical, nuther!

" Blamed ol' blunderhead! couldn't he see
'T the poor I was marciful tu meant me?
But here he goes on, in a gushin' mood,
To tell o' the woman's gratitude,
Because I've been so exceedingly good
 As to pity her sad condition,
An' give him the blessed authority tu
Remit — remit — the rent that is due.
Why don't he remit, then? wish I knew!
'Stid o' that, here's more of his hullabalew,
 To thank me for the remission!

" Remission — remit. Oh, drat the dunce!"
 And he rushed for a dictionary:
It having occurred to him all at once
 That the meanings sometimes vary
Of even the simplest word we write;
And that a prosy old parson might
Use one, and a man of business quite
 Another. vocabulary.

Finger and eye ran down the page:
" R, a — R, e " —he was flushed with rage :
" Remember — Remind — Remit ! " — at last
The terrible talon had it fast,
With the definition against it set :
" Send back," he read ; but, lower yet.
" To release, to forgive, as a sin or a debt ! "
Ah, through that mesh in the treacherous net
        Had slipped the widow's pittance !
'Twas so ! 'twas strange ! 'twas very absurd,
That thus from a phrase, or a single word,
With equal reason could be inferred
        Collection of debt, or quittance !
Words have their forks, like highways, whence
To left and right run the roads of sense ;
And, taking the wrong derivative,
The heedless old parson had come to give
        Remission instead of remittance.

Elkanah glared for a moment, and then,
With a snort at the book, and a scoff at the men
Who invented the language, seized his pen,
Tore one letter, and wrote again,
    Protruding his chin, while the hard dry grin
        Grew terribly savage and sinister ;
Till, too impatient to brook delay,

He quite forgot it was Christmas-day,
Swung on his ulster, and swooped away
   Toward Tannery Town and the Widow Brown
     And the good old blundering minister.

As out by the forenoon train he went,
     He had ample time to consider:
" To be soft-soaped to sich an extent —
Cracked up like a spavined hoss that's meant
     To be sold to the highest bidder —
It's pooty dumbed rough on a plain old gent
That never was known to give a cent,
Say nothin' o' seventy dollars' rent,
     To anybody's widder!
An' I ain't one o' the kind that cares
To be boosted up in a woman's prayers
     Fer a favor I never did her.

" Yet she might pray fer me all her days,
An' I wouldn't object to the parson's praise,
     Which he spreads so thick in his letter;
But though he believes it himself, and though
Other folks may think it's all jes' so,
     The plague is, I know better!
He'll wonder what sort of a beast I be,

When I tell him square out how it seemed to me,
What a blamed, ridickelous fool's idee,
        That I should forgive a debtor!"

Quick moist flushes, strange hot streaks,
Shot down to his shins and up to his cheeks.
He loosened his collar, and wondered what
In time made 'em keep the cars so hot.
Still, as he thought of the interview
He was going to seek, the warmer he grew.
And he said to himself, with a leer, " Must be
I'm fond of parsons' s'ciety!
Fer what else under the canopy
I'm makin' the trip fer, I can't see ;
Sence a letter or tu would as soon undu
        The snarl he's got me inter,
Save railroad fare, an' the wear an' tear
        Of a journey in midwinter.

" It's an awk'ard mess, I du declare!
The widder she'll cry, an' the parson he'll stare,
An' like enough somebody else will swear —
Wish I was back in my office chair!
Fer why should I go twelve mile or so
        An' lose my time an' my dinner,

To prove to their face, beyond a doubt,
'T I ain't no saint, as they make out,
    But a hardened sort of a sinner ? ''

Some such thoughts perplexed his brain,
As up to the station rolled the train,
With slackening speed and brakes screwed down,
And the brakeman bawled out, '' Tannery Town ! ''
'' Wa'al, here I be ! '' With a gathering frown
And firm-set teeth, old Elkanah straight
Took his way to the parson's gate ;
No longer inclined to turn about,
    In a flurry of confusion,
And like a coward retrace his route,
But grimly resolved to carry out
    His original resolution.
Though, after all, he approached the spot,
Outwardly cold and inwardly hot,
As a brave man goes to be hanged or shot,
Or whatever else he thinks is not
    The thing for his constitution.
And when this answer he received,
'' Parson ain't to hum '' — will it be believed ?
He felt like the very same man reprieved
    At the moment of execution.

Wa'al, no, he wouldn't go in and wait;
He stood in the snow at the parsonage gate:
No train back till half-past one,
And the village bells had just begun
To ring for noon : for a minute or two
He stood, uncertain what to do,
Looking doubtfully up and down
The dreary streets of Tannery Town,
And thought of his money and Mrs. Brown :
　　　Then this is what he did do —
He turned his feet up the snowy street,
　　　And went to call on the widow.

'Twas Christmas-time, as I said before ;
And when, arrived at the cottage door,
　　　He reached for the old bell handle,
He paused a moment, amazed and grim,
For he heard such a racket as seemed to him,
In the home of the late lamented Jim,
　　　Sufficient cause for scandal.

A short, sharp ring : then a hurried noise
Of whispering, scampering girls and boys ;
And the door was opened a little space,
Through which peered out, with a bashful grace,
　　　A surprisingly pretty-looking,

Timidly smiling, bright young blonde ;
And Elkanah caught, from the room beyond,
   A savory sniff, a wonderful whiff,
      Of most delicious cooking.

He sees a table, with neat cloth spread,
Steaming dishes, and cream-white bread ;
Cranberry sauce, and thick squash pies ;
And the curly brown pates and wondering eyes
      Of the imps that had made the clatter ;
Then the mother just bringing in, to crown
Her banquet, a beautiful, golden-brown,
      Great roasted goose on a platter.

A crabbed old man, to whom the sight
Of happy children gave small delight ;
A hungry man, who had come so far
To a feast his presence could only mar ;
      An iron-fisted miser,
Who would seldom afford himself a fat,
Delectable Christmas goose like that,
Or indulge in anything half so good —
Confronting the widow, there he stood,
      Just showing one grim incisor ;
And it certainly seemed that his presence would —
      To say the least — surprise her.

For he said to himself, "Her means are spent,
An' she hasn't a penny to pay her rent!
  While this is the way she gorges
Her ravenous tribe on the fat of the land.
I'll let her know that I understand
  Whose money pays fer the orgies!"

But, seeing the old man standing there,
The widow, seemingly unaware
  Of his brow's severe contraction;
Perceiving only his thin white hair,
And his almost venerable air,
Wiped her fingers, and placed a chair,
  With a charmingly natural action;
Welcoming him with never a trace
Of guile in her smiling and grateful face;
Accounting this visit the crowning grace
  Of his noble benefaction.

"O, sir!" she began, "I am glad you are here" —
With a quivering lip and a starting tear —
"To see what happiness" (this was gall
To the stingy old wretch) "you have given us all!
Since you were so good" — "Not I," he cried;
"I never was good!"   But she replied,
  With gentle, sweet insistence:

" It seems but a trifle to you, no doubt;
Such kindness as yours " — Here he burst out,
" I tell ye, woman, ye're talkin' about
    A thing that has no existence."

" Ah, you may say that, since you have shown
A goodness which you are too good to own!
But I could never, with what I know,
Permit another to wrong you so."
Then up spoke one of the younger crew :
" Ye may bet yer dollars on that! it's true ;
For only yesterday, I tell you,
    Wasn't she in high dudgeon,
Just hearing you called by Deacon Shaw
The keenest old skinflint ever he saw!
He said he would sooner have hoped to draw
Sap from a hatchet or blood from a straw,
Than money that wasn't allowed by law,
    From such an old curmudgeon.

"Well, what have I said ?"   "Hush, Jamie, hush!"
    Cries the mother, in consternation ;
While Elkanah starts, with an angry flush
    And a vigorous exclamation.
" Did he say that ? — say that of me?
He's tighter himself than the bark of a tree."

" He has more heart than he lets folks see :
A little like you in that," says she.
" Ho! ho! wa'al, wa'al! that's a queer idee!
     That's a curi's ca'calation!'"

" But he, when at last he understood
What a friend you had been, how exceedingly good,
To my poor orphans," she went on,
" And me — for the sake of him that is gone —
He was humbled; he took it quite to heart;
Declared you had acted a noble part,
     And expressed sincere repentance
For having misjudged you so till now.
But your example " —   " Example! I vow,
Mis' Brown," snarls Elkanah ; but somehow
     He couldn't complete the sentence.

" Your Christian example!" the widow cries,
" Who wants proof of it, there it lies " —
With a glance of pride at the great squash pies,
     And the goose superbly basted.
" The deacon was here at half-past one ;
And at half-past two the proof had begun :
The goose was brought by the deacon's son,
And then it seemed as if every one
Must do as the deacon and you had done."

"'HO! HO! WA'AL, WA'AL! THAT'S A QUEER IDEE!
THAT'S A CURUS CALCALATION!'"

" Yes, sir," says Jamie ; " and wasn't it fun!
It was ring, ring, ring! it was run, run, run !
Squashes that weighed pretty nigh a ton !
     Such apples you never tasted ! "
" It came to us in our sorest need,"
The widow resumed ; " and all are agreed
'Twas a harvest of which you sowed the seed.
You see your charity was, indeed,
     An example that wasn't wasted."

"My charity!" Elkanah groaned. " Well, well!"
" 'Twas more of a blessing than I can tell ; " —
She choked a little and wiped a tear —
" For we have been dreadfully poor this year.
'Tis a hard, hard struggle to provide
For my five little ones since he died.
Faithfully, every day, I meant
To save a little to pay my rent;
I stinted and planned, but still I found,
As often as Saturday night came round.
I had spared, when they were patched and fed,
Hardly enough for Sunday's bread.
Such constant weariness, want and care
Seemed often more than a life could bear.
Then came, oh ! sir, your gracious gift,
Which all of a sudden seemed to lift

The burden which weighed me to the ground ;
And all these other good friends came round ;
And so, in our joy and thankfulness,
It seemed to me 1 could do no less
Than make a feast," she said with a smile.
" Be patient ! be quiet ! "   For all the while
       The hungry children clamored,
And climbed the chairs, and peeped at the pies,
And ogled the goose with wistful eyes.
" 'Tis a favor," said she, " 1 should greatly prize,
If you would sit by, and not despise
The bounty which Heaven through you supplies."
" Hem ! wa'al ! ye take me by surprise.
       Don't know," the old man stammered.

She smilingly reached for his coat and hat,
And the goose was fragrant, the goose was fat.
" I think you will stay."   " Wa'al, as to that,
       I don't dine out very often ;
I called to explain — but never mind.
Fact is, Mis' Brown, I haven't dined ;
And if you insist — sence you air so kind " —
He was rather surprised himself to find
       His heart beginning to soften.

" Don't care 'f I du."   And down he sat.
The goose was fragrant, the goose was fat.

The old man did the carving;
The sauce was dished, the gravy poured,
And the plates all round that little board
Were filled in a manner that didn't afford
    The slightest hint of starving.

Not in all that dreary year
Had her cottage known such cheer.
With hope, and her happy children near,
    The widow smiled contented.
Even old Elkanah ceased to be
Greatly scandalized to see
Cheerful faces and childish glee
    In the home of the late lamented.

Nature's ways are wise and kind :
Clouds pass, dawn breaks. and ever behind
Each dark sea hollow swells a wave ;
And fresh grass grows on the new-made grave;
And softly over the broken heart.
    And its sorrowful recollections.
The leaves of another hope will start,
    And tender new affections.

The widow talked and told her plans :
What a dutiful child was Nance!
The parson had got her boys a chance

To blow the organ the coming year :
" So there will be twenty dollars clear !
The girls will help me more and more;
I'll sew ; and often, as heretofore,
Earn bread for the morrow while they sleep;
And so I have hopes that I yet may keep
        My little flock together —
With Heaven so kind and friends so good —
Send them to school, and provide them food
        And shelter them from the weather.

" But oh ! what a change for them and me ;
How different now it all would be,
If my dear husband " — Mrs. Brown
Here, for some reason, quite broke down ;
And even old Elkanah's sight grew weak ;
You might have observed in his withered cheek
        Some unaccustomed twitches,
And in his voice, when he tried to speak,
        Some very unusual hitches ;
For, seeing how long she yet must strain
Her utmost energies, just to gain
Bread for her babes — perhaps in vain —
He had some twinges of shame and pain,
And a curious feeling I can't explain,
        At the thought of his hoarded riches.

" Hem! wa'al, Mis' Brown! it's a pooty tough case! "
He made a motion as if to place
His hand in his pocket, but drew it back.
" Though I must say, you've got a knack!
You're gittin' along, an' I'm dreffle glad!
No more, no, thank'ee, ma'am! I hain't had
Sich a dinner as this, I don't know when! "
Down went the uncertain hand again.
      " Your children are well, an' growin';
Few years, your boys 'll be rich men —
      Mabby they will, no knowin'."
He merely pushed back his empty plate,
Then tugged at his watch. " Ha! is it so late?
I'd no i'dee on't! train won't wait;
      Guess I'll haf ter be goin'! "

" Must you, indeed! How the time has flown! "
The lonely old man had never known
So grateful a soul, a look and tone
      So gentle and so caressing;
And while she handed his hat and coat,
Arranged the collar about his throat,
Smoothed the creases, and brushed his arm,
He felt a strange, bewildering charm,
The very touch of her hand shed such
      Unconscious love and blessing!

" I thought there was something he came to say,
To explain!" cries Jamie.   "Ah, yes! by the way!"
        Says Elkanah, slightly flurried ;
" A leetle mistake — but that's all right !
The parson. he didn't take in, not quite,
My full intent regardin' the rent :
        Don't be the least mite worried
'Bout that fer sartin another year. —
Bless me ! I b'lieve it's the train I hear !
        Good-day ! " And off he hurried.

He seemed surrounded and pursued
By spirits of joy and gratitude !
And he said to himself, " I must conclude.
Although the ol' parson wa'n't very shrewd,
        'Twas a lucky mistake o' his'n ! "
And he felt some most surprising things,
Strange perturbations and flutterings,
As of something within him spreading wings —
        The angel within, new-risen !

" I'm beat if there ain't the parson now ! "
With eager stride and radiant brow
The minister crossed a steep by-street,
Through ridges of snow leg-deep, to greet
The friend of the widow and fatherless,

Who growled to himself, "Good thing, I guess,
Fer some of the fatherless folks we know,
Me and him didn't meet an hour ago —
  Good thing all round, shouldn't wonder!"
The parson came panting up the hill,
Hands out, with a greeting of warm good-will;
All smiles; serenely unconscious still
  Of his most amazing blunder.

A soul as simple as rills that run
Joyous and clear in the summer sun!
Not one who had chosen his work, but one
  The Lord Himself had chosen;
A child of faith, and a shepherd indeed;
Not one of those whose formal creed
Has the tinkling sound and the hollow look
Of ice left over a shrunken brook —
Shrunken away from the living day,
  Leaving its surface frozen.

Under the leafless village elms
The parson waylays and overwhelms
  With more felicitation
Of the late epistolary sort
The impatient old man, who cuts him short
  With a quaint gesticulation.

“ No more o’ that, please understand !
I’ve seen Jim’s widder.”   This time the hand
Dives into the pocket, and brings out
A bright bank-note : “ Guess the’ ain’t no doubt
But what we’d oughter give her a lift ;
An’ here’s a trifle, a Christmas gift,
     I was pooty nigh fergittin’.
Remit her rent the comin’ year ;
And I’d like to remit to her now this ’ere.
By the way !” drawls he, with a sidelong leer,
“ Did j’ever notice — it’s kind o’ queer —
     There’s tew ways o’ remittin’ ? ”

www.ingramcontent.com/pod-product-compliance
Lightning Source LLC
Chambersburg PA
CBHW021122020726

47500CB00003B/875